# THE
# DRAGON
# NANNY

## C.L.G. MARTIN

*Illustrated by*

## ROBERT RAYEVSKY

Macmillan Publishing Company   New York
Collier Macmillan Publishers   London

Macmillan Publishing Company
866 Third Avenue, New York, NY 10022
Collier Macmillan Canada, Inc.
Printed and bound by South China Printing Company, Hong Kong
First American Edition

10 9 8 7 6 5 4 3 2 1

The text of this book is set in 14 point Goudy Old Style.
The illustrations are rendered in ink and watercolor.
Library of Congress Cataloging-in-Publication Data
Martin, C. L. G. The dragon nanny.
Summary: An elderly woman who loses her
job as a caretaker to the king's children
ends up taking care of a dragon family.
[1. Dragons—Fiction] I. Rayevsky, Robert, ill. II. Title.
PZ7.M356776Dr  1988  [E]  87-7674
ISBN 0-02-762440-4

With love and thanks,
to my very special
mom and dad
—C.L.G.M.


To my mother
—R.R.

Nightfall brought a chilly dampness to the forest. The underbrush crackled with unseen creatures, while skeleton trees danced in the wind.

Nanny Nell Hannah listened. Her plump little body trembled, and her teeth would not stop chattering. Nanny was very frightened—but not of the darkness.

"What shall I do? Whatever shall I do?" Nanny sobbed. Slumping down on a spongy bed of moss, she hiccuped and blew her nose loudly.

"Silence!" thundered a monstrous voice from the blackness. "Who dares to disturb my sleep?"

Nanny's heart flopped over backward. She stared into two glowing red eyes, unable to move. "I—I am N-N-Nanny N-N-Nell Hannah, nanny to the royal nursery ... er, former nanny. The king fired me because he thinks I'm too old. Now I have nowhere to go and—"

"Enough!" The glowing red eyes moved, and a huge, angry dragon emerged from the shadows. "No one trespasses in Dragonia's forest. Prepare to die!"

"Go ahead," Nanny said. "Do what you must. I am no use to anyone, anyway."

Dragonia stopped. "That's it? Aren't you going to beg for your life? Aren't you going to fight? Aren't you at least going to get mad?"

"Oh, no," Nanny answered weakly. "I never get angry." She held her breath and closed her eyes.

"Goo-goo, Mama. Da-ga-boo-goo."

Nanny opened one eye, then the other. From behind Dragonia's enormous tail peeked two baby dragons.

"Oh, good grief. Now look what you've done. I will be up all night. Sparky! Cinder! You go back to sleep this minute," Dragonia scolded. "Mama has business to take care of." She smiled wickedly at Nanny.

Nanny gulped. "Wait! If you spare me I can be very useful to you."

"How could you possibly be of use to me?" Dragonia snorted. "Except perhaps as a midnight snack."

"Why, as a nanny, of course. You would be free to sleep or wander the forest, doing whatever it is you dragons do. I would take wonderful care of your children."

Sparky and Cinder watched the grown-ups curiously.

"Hmmm," said Dragonia. "Very well. We will try you out, Nanny Nell Hannah. If you perform your tasks well, you will live. If you fail, I will enjoy a tasty treat." And with a chuckle, Dragonia disappeared into her cave.

Nanny's eyes met the children's. "Bedtime," she said.

Nanny rose before the morning sun. She piled armfuls of scratchy firewood higher and higher around the dragon-sized baby bottles.

"Breakfast will be ready soon, dears," she called.

The sleepy dragons poked their heads out of the cave.

Nanny climbed onto a boulder to tie on their bibs. She gasped. "Oh, dear, how will I ever manage to lift your heavy bottles way up here?"

Dragonia looked on in silence, lazily licking her lips. And the babies were getting restless.

Nanny caught sight of a thick vine. She grabbed it, tied it to a bottle, threw the end over a high branch, and tugged and pulled until the bottle fit neatly into the fork in the tree. "Phew! This job is not going to be easy," she said, hoisting the second bottle into place.

Cinder and Sparky drank their breakfast happily. Dragonia fell back to sleep, a frown across her giant brow.

Week after week Nanny worked hard under Dragonia's watchful eyes. Burping baby dragons was not a simple chore. Not to mention diapering them! And rocking them to sleep! But Nanny always found a way.

Then one day the mother dragon made a big announcement. "You have been lucky so far, Nanny Nell Hannah," she said. "Now the time has come to teach the children fire breathing. All you have to do is make them very angry, and the rest will come naturally." Dragonia's eyes twinkled, and her mouth twisted into a queer smile.

"All right, children, pay attention," Nanny
instructed. "Today we are going to learn fire breathing.
Sparky, think of something that makes you really mad."

Sparky just turned somersaults and stood on his head.

Nanny made an ugly face at Cinder, but the little
dragon laughed and licked Nanny's cheek. It was no use.

As the days passed, Dragonia began to lose patience. "I will give you one more week, Nanny Nell Hannah," she warned. "If in that time you have not taught my children to breathe fire, you shall be my Sunday dinner."

Nanny said to herself, "This will be the end of me." But at the same moment an idea began to take shape in her head.

While the mother dragon slept, Nanny crept into the forest. She collected branches and vines and fastened them together in odd shapes. She used animal skins and bones left over from Dragonia's dinner to make two large bellows. With a sharp rock she hollowed out a fallen tree.

By daybreak a peculiar contraption stood before her. "I hope this works," Nanny said.

Nanny waited breathlessly for Dragonia to leave. When the huge dragon was finally out of sight, Nanny pushed her strange invention deep inside the cave. There she built a fire.

Up, down, up, down she pumped the great bellows. The fire grew into a roaring flame and leaped out of the cave. Quickly Nanny blew the second bellows into the hollow log. Out came an evil, rumbling growl.

Cinder and Sparky giggled excitedly at this wonderful joke.

The smoke and flame brought Dragonia hurrying
from the forest. Nanny and the babies were waiting,
resting in the sunshine.

"You did it!" said the mother dragon proudly. "You
finally breathed fire. And so well, too." She turned to
Nanny. "Once again you are lucky, Nanny Nell Hannah."

Nanny took a deep breath.

"Come, children," Dragonia called eagerly. "We are going on our first outing together in the countryside. Now that you are fire-breathing dragons, you will be perfectly safe."

As the dragon family strolled toward the village, Nanny felt strangely guilty—and worried.

Before long the dragon alarm screamed its warning across the valley. Nanny watched helplessly from the mountain cave as the villagers raced for their weapons.

Dragonia seemed unconcerned. She reared back her head and spat a sizzling flame over the crowd. Smiling confidently, she waited for her children to do the same.

"Oh, the poor babies," Nanny wailed. Sparky hid behind his mother, burying his face in her tail. Cinder tried to escape but in her terror fled toward the town.

People scattered in front of the little dragon, until they noticed that Cinder wasn't breathing fire. Why, she wasn't even growling. She was actually afraid of *them*.

Unable to leave Sparky, Dragonia watched as Cinder was taken prisoner and led away to the castle. Dragonia's red eyes blazed up at the mountain. "You will pay, Nanny Nell Hannah," the dragon roared. "You will pay!"

Nanny knew she was to blame for Cinder's capture. Petrified, she faced the furious mother.

"You tricked me!" Dragonia shrieked. "My baby is locked away in a dark dungeon because you tricked me. Now you *shall* die!" She took a deep breath and threw back her head.

"W-w-wait," Nanny begged. "I will rescue Cinder. I have a plan."

Dashing into the cave, Nanny ripped apart her fire-breathing machine. She rewrapped the branches and vines into a heavy box. This she dragged and heaved onto the hollow log. Then she stitched frantically on the great bellows. There was no time to rest.

Finally Nanny hobbled from the cave, an old peddler woman pushing her cart. A ragged shawl was tied around her head, and above her cart hung a huge animal skin umbrella.

"Nanny Nell Hannah," Dragonia growled, "what are you doing?"

"No time to explain," Nanny muttered as she trudged down the mountainside.

"Do not try to trick me again, Nanny Nell Hannah. Nowhere will you be safe from me," the dragon screamed.

At the castle gates no one noticed the peddler woman. She went directly to the dungeon, nervously keeping one eye out for guards.

"Don't worry, Cinder," she whispered. "Nanny is here. I'm going to get you out, dear."

Quickly Nanny took apart the peddler's pushcart. She was so busy reassembling her fire-breathing machine that she failed to hear footsteps approaching.

"Well, what have we here?" a gruff voice snickered.

"Looks to me like this little lady is trying to rescue our dragon," said another. "We'll see about that."

The guards grabbed Nanny roughly by the arms. But even as she struggled she noticed that black smoke had begun to puff from Cinder's nostrils.

"Put the dragon lover in chains," ordered one guard.

Cinder growled. She took a deep breath and blew a streak of fire across the dungeon. "I did it, Nanny! I did it!" She squealed with delight.

"Yes, dear. We'll talk about it later." Nanny pushed the little dragon ahead of her, and in the smoky confusion the pair escaped.

Heart pounding, Nanny glanced over her shoulder. The guards were running for their horses. Even the king had joined the chase. "Stop them!" he cried.

The guards whipped their horses to breakneck speed. Pounding hooves swirled the dusty road into a charging tornado.

The dragon cave was now in sight, and Nanny could see Dragonia's fierce glare. "Run to Mama, Cinder," she said, panting.

Nanny sat on the ground. She was too tired to
move. She was also sick and tired of Dragonia's anger.

The guards rushed closer and closer. "Traitor!" they
shouted. "Dragon lover! Off with her head."

The king was in the lead. "Nanny Nell Hannah, it's
you!" he cried. "How could *you* become a traitor?"

Nanny felt strange. Her cheeks grew hot. Her eyes flashed as she jumped to her feet. "Just one minute!" she yelled. "How *dare* you call me a traitor. You *fired* me after I served you faithfully all those years. Then I found a home with the little dragons. I taught them to be loving and gentle, and they were almost killed because of it. Now Dragonia wants to turn me into a Nanny-burger, and you want to chop off my head. Well, I've had enough of all of you! I'm leaving!"

"Good grief," Dragonia mumbled. "We need you, Nanny Nell Hannah. Come back to us ... please."

"Oh, no!" cried the king. "*I* need you, Nanny Nell Hannah. The royal nursery is a shambles. Why, just

yesterday my little princesses sewed their new nanny to the sofa. Please come back to us. Anyway, people belong with people, not with dragons."

"Why?" Sparky demanded indignantly.

"Because dragons and people are enemies."

"Why?" Cinder echoed.

"Because! That's why!" the king snapped. "Nanny Nell Hannah, come back to the royal nursery, and I will grant you any wish!"

Cinder sniffled sadly, and Sparky pouted and stamped his foot.

Nanny grinned. "*Any* wish?"

The next day a strange and shocking sight greeted visitors to the little kingdom. An enormous dragon with glowing red eyes peered out over the castle gates. Around her neck hung a shiny silver shield that proclaimed her CAPTAIN OF THE GUARD.

Unseen by outside eyes, the captain's tail made a perfect slide for lively little princes and princesses, and for little dragons. Together they skipped rope and learned their ABCs—all under the watchful, loving eyes of a very able dragon nanny.

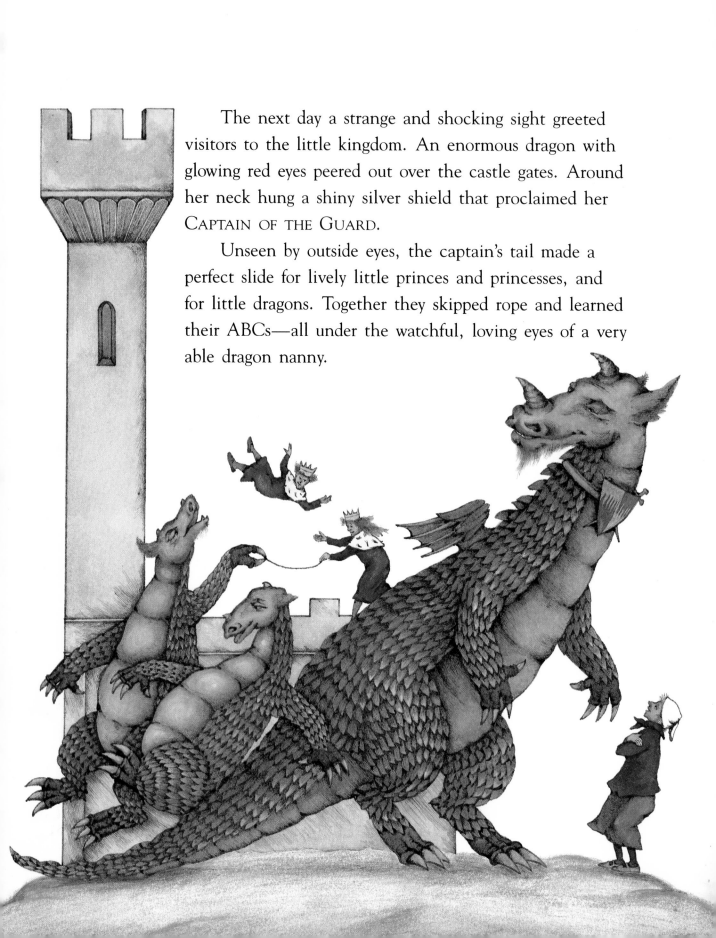